RICHARD SCARRY'S
To Market, To Market

A MOTHER GOOSE BOOK
of Good Things to
SCRATCH and SNIFF

gb Golden Press • New York
Western Publishing Company, Inc.
Racine, Wisconsin

To market, to market, to buy a fat pig,
Home again, home again, jiggety-jig;

To market, to market, to buy a fat hog,
Home again, home again, jiggety-jog.

Simple Simon met a pieman,
Going to the fair;
Says Simple Simon to the pieman,
"Let me taste your ware."

Says the pieman to Simple Simon,
"Show me first your penny."
Says Simple Simon to the pieman,
"Indeed I have not any."

Tom, Tom, the piper's son,
Stole a pig and away did run.
The pig was eat, and Tom was beat,
And Tom went crying down the street.

Tom, Tom, of whom you've read,
Loved the smell of gingerbread.
Scratch and sniff; you'll like it, too.
Now wasn't that great fun to do?

GINGERBREAD PIGS

Sing a song of sixpence,
A pocket full of rye;
Four and twenty blackbirds
Baked in a pie!

When the pie was opened,
The birds began to sing;
Wasn't that a dainty dish
To set before the King?

The King was in his counting-house,
Counting out his money;
The Queen was in the parlor,
Eating bread and honey.

The maid was in the garden,
Hanging out the clothes;
Along came a blackbird,
And snipped off her nose!

9

Blow, wind, blow! and go, mill, go!
That the miller may grind his corn;
That the baker may take it,
And into bread make it,
And bring us a loaf in the morn.

Little Jack Horner
Sat in the corner,
Eating a Christmas pie;
He put in his thumb,
And pulled out a plum,
And said, "What a good boy am I!"

*Scratch-a-cake, sniff-a-cake,
my little cook;
Smell the banana cake
here in this book.*

Pat-a-cake, pat-a-cake, baker's man,
Bake me a cake as fast as you can;
Pat it and prick it, and mark it with B,
And put it in the oven for Baby and me.

Little Poll Parrot
Sat in his garret,
Eating toast and tea.
A little brown mouse
Jumped into the house,
And stole it all away.

Little Tommy Tucker
Sings for his supper.
What shall we give him?
White bread and butter.

How shall he cut it
Without a knife?
How will he be married
Without a wife?

Polly put the kettle on,
Polly put the kettle on,
Polly put the kettle on,
We'll all have tea.

Sukey take it off again,
Sukey take it off again,
Sukey take it off again,
They've all gone away.

13

Jack Sprat could eat no fat,
His wife could eat no lean,
And so between them both, you see,
They licked the platter clean.

Scratch, scratch the sausage fat,
And this is what you'll smell:
Sausage meat that's spicey sweet.
I know you'll like it well.

15

Old Mother Hubbard
Went to the cupboard
To fetch her poor dog a bone;
But when she came there,
The cupboard was bare,
And so the poor dog had none.

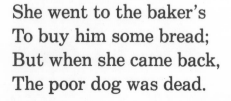

She went to the baker's
To buy him some bread;
But when she came back,
The poor dog was dead.

She went to the undertaker's
To buy him a coffin;
But when she came back,
The poor dog was laughing.

She took a clean dish
To get him some tripe;
But when she came back,
He was smoking a pipe.

She went to the grocer's
To buy him some fruit;
But when she came back,
He was playing the flute.

She went to the tailor's
To buy him a coat;
But when she came back,
He was riding a goat.

She went to the hatter's
To buy him a hat;
But when she came back,
He was feeding the cat.

She went to the barber's
To buy him a wig;
But when she came back,
He was dancing a jig.

She went to the seamstress
To buy him some linen;
But when she came back,
The dog was a-spinning.

She went to the cobbler's
To buy him some shoes;
But when she came back,
He was reading the news.

She went to the hosier's
To buy him some hose;
But when she came back,
He was dressed in his clothes.

The dame made a curtsey,
The dog made a bow;
The dame said, "Your servant."
The dog said, "Bow-wow."

Peter Piper picked a peck of pickled peppers;
A peck of pickled peppers Peter Piper picked.
If Peter Piper picked a peck of pickled peppers,
Where's the peck of pickled peppers Peter Piper picked?

Pussycat, pussycat,
Wilt thou be mine?
Thou shalt not wash dishes
Nor yet feed the swine,
But sit on a cushion
And sew a fine seam
And feed upon strawberries,
Sugar and cream.

Little Miss Muffet
Sat on a tuffet,
Eating her curds and whey;
There came a big spider,
Who sat down beside her,
And frightened Miss Muffet away.

Little maid, pretty maid, whither goest thou?
Down in the meadow to milk my cow.
Shall I go with thee? No, not now;
When I send for thee, then come thou.

21

Three little kittens, they lost their mittens,
And they began to cry,
"Oh, mother dear, we sadly fear,
Our mittens we have lost."

"What! Lost your mittens, you naughty kittens!
Then you shall have no pie."
"Mee-ow, mee-ow, mee-ow."
"No, you shall have no pie."

The three little kittens, they found their mittens,
And they began to cry,
"Oh, mother dear, see here, see here,
Our mittens we have found."

"Put on your mittens, you silly kittens,
And you shall have some pie."
"Purr-r, purr-r, purr-r,
Oh, let us have some pie."

The three little kittens put on their mittens,
And soon ate up the pie;
"Oh, mother dear, we greatly fear
Our mittens we have soiled."

"What! Soiled your mittens, you naughty kittens!"
Then they began to sigh,
"Mee-ow, mee-ow, mee-ow."
Then they began to sigh.

The three little kittens, they washed their mittens,
And hung them out to dry;
"Oh, mother dear, do you not hear
Our mittens we have washed?"

"What! Washed your mittens, you good little kittens?
But I smell a rat close by."
"Mee-ow, mee-ow, mee-ow.
We smell a rat close by."

The kittens three, as you can see,
Couldn't wait to try;
Oh, reader dear, scratch here, scratch here,
And sniff this lemon pie.

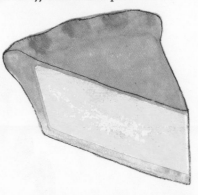

23

Little Boy Blue,
Come blow your horn,
The sheep's in the meadow,
The cow's in the corn.

But where is the little boy
Tending the sheep?
He's under a haycock,
Fast asleep.

Will you wake him?
No, not I.
For if I do,
He's sure to cry.

This little pig likes oranges,
This little pig scratched one,
This little pig went sniff, sniff, sniff;
You try it, too—it's fun!

This little pig went to market,

This little pig stayed home.

This little pig had roast beef,

This little pig had none.

And this little pig cried, "Wee-wee-wee-wee-wee,"
All the way home.

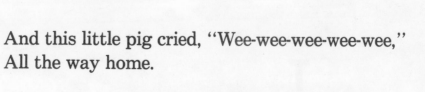

The Queen of Hearts,
She made some tarts,
All on a summer's day.
The Knave of Hearts,
He stole the tarts,
And took them clean away.

The King of Hearts
Called for the tarts,
And beat the Knave full sore.
The Knave of Hearts
Brought back the tarts,
And vowed he'd steal no more.

The Queen of Hearts
Got back her tarts,
And served them all for tea.
Scratch these hearts—
Sweet strawberry tarts
Smell tasty as can be.